PUFFIN BOOKS

The Weekly Ghost

Toby Forward was born in Coventry. He went to college to pursue theological training and subsequently became a parish priest. He is now a full-time writer and lives with his wife and two daughters near Hull.

Other books by Toby Forward

THE TOAD LADY
TRAVELLING BACKWARDS

WYVERN WINTER
WYVERN SPRING
WYVERN SUMMER
WYVERN FALL

The Weekly Ghost

Toby Forward

Illustrated by David Axtell

PUFFIN BOOKS

For Rosalind and Timothy

PUFFIN BOOKS

Published by the Penguin Group
Penguin Books Ltd, 27 Wrights Lane, London W8 5TZ, England
Penguin Books USA Inc., 375 Hudson Street, New York, New York 10014, USA
Penguin Books Australia Ltd, Ringwood, Victoria, Australia
Penguin Books Canada Ltd, 10 Alcorn Avenue, Toronto, Ontario, Canada M4V 3B2
Penguin Books (NZ) Ltd, 182–190 Wairau Road, Auckland 10, New Zealand

Penguin Books Ltd, Registered Offices: Harmondsworth, Middlesex, England

First published by Andersen Press Limited 1995
Published in Puffin Books 1996
1 3 5 7 9 10 8 6 4 2

Text copyright © Toby Forward, 1995
Illustrations copyright © David Axtell, 1995
All rights reserved

The moral right of the author has been asserted

Made and printed in Great Britain by Clays Ltd, St Ives plc

Chapter 1

Stephanie stared around the classroom in amazement.

'It's all different,' she said.

'Is it?' asked David. He scratched a very tousled head and made the hair look even worse. 'I didn't notice.'

'When did this come?' Stephanie pointed at the tank of goldfish.

'Weeks ago,' said David.

'Two weeks,' said Jasvinda.

'Is that all?' said David. 'I thought it had always been there.'

'And where's Peanuts?' Stephanie asked. 'I've brought him some food.'

Joey threw his bag on to his chair and pushed Stephanie out of the way. 'Oh,' he said. 'You're back,' and he grinned at her.

Stephanie grinned back.

'Peanuts is dead,' he said.

Stephanie's grin dropped from her bright face. Jasvinda took Stephanie's arm.

'We haven't got a hamster now,' she explained. 'We've got goldfish.'

'I hate goldfish,' said Stephanie. 'I want Peanuts.' She was close to tears.

'Who says we have to have goldfish?'

'Miss Evans,' said David.

'Who?' demanded Stephanie, her distress beginning to turn to anger. Just then the door swung open and a large woman in a huge loose frock walked in. She closed it behind her very quietly, as though a noise would make a bomb go off, and she walked to the teacher's desk. At once, everyone stopped talking and stood behind their chairs. Stephanie tried to stand near to David and Jasvinda and Joey because they were her best friends and they always stayed together, but there wasn't a free chair at that table so she had to stand in a space.

'Sit down, please,' said Miss Evans, in a very quiet voice. The class all sat, still in silence. Stephanie couldn't believe it.

'Hello,' she said. 'I haven't got a chair. I always sit here. I'll just . . .'

'Silence,' said the large lady, still in the very small voice. Stephanie stopped. 'There is a chair for you at that table.' Miss Evans pointed to the other side of the room. 'And a tray with your name on it ready for you. We have been expecting you.' Miss Evans looked at a piece of paper with Stephanie's name

6

on it and some other writing.

Stephanie looked at where Miss Evans was pointing. It was the table where Janine sat. Janine was wet and said things like 'Who's your boy friend, Stephanie?'

'No,' said Stephanie. 'I always sit here. I don't sit with ...' She couldn't say Janine so she stumbled and ended up by mumbling something that Miss Evans couldn't really hear. But Miss Evans didn't mind.

'So, just squeeze through and sit there next to Janine.' There was no choice. Stephanie squeezed through and sat down.

'Who is she?' she hissed to Clive on the other side of her. She didn't like Clive a lot either, but he was better than Janine. Clive stared ahead and didn't answer. They were all doing the same.

'David,' said Miss Evans. 'Have you got a comb? You look like a scarecrow.'

'No, Miss Evans,' said David.

'See me at playtime,' she told him. David scratched his head and nodded. 'Today, children,' said Miss Evans, 'we welcome Stephanie to our class. Now, Stephanie has been in Jamaica for a wedding and is joining us late in the term, but we all want to make her feel very welcome. So please say, "Welcome home, Stephanie." '

Stephanie could not believe her ears. All the class,

including Joey and Jasvinda and David joined in in a slow monotonous chant of 'Welcome home, Stephanie.'

Stephanie buried her face in her hands and didn't know where to look.

'And now,' said Miss Evans, 'we'd like Stephanie to come to the front of the class and introduce herself to us and say what it has been like enjoying all that lovely Jamaican sun while we've been shivering here in England.' And she would not allow Stephanie to refuse.

At playtime, Stephanie hurled herself out of the classroom, steaming with anger and impatience. She ran to the other side of the yard and waited for her friends to come to her.

'Who is she?' she shouted. 'And where's Miss Markworthy?'

'She left,' said Joey. 'She's having a baby.'

'A baby?' said Stephanie. 'But she didn't tell us.'

'Yes she did,' said Jasvinda. 'We had a collection and bought her a present.'

'And she gave us a bar of chocolate each when she left,' said David.

'And she's going to come in and see us,' said Jasvinda.

'When the baby's born,' said David.

'And show him to us,' said Joey.

'Or her,' said Jasvinda.

'Or her.'

'Look,' said Stephanie. 'This is terrible. I've only been away about three weeks and everything's changed. The classroom is all moved about. Peanuts is dead. We've got goldfish. I have to sit next to Wet Janine. Miss Markworthy's gone to have a baby. This Miss Whatshername has taken over. And everyone's so quiet.'

'And we don't go swimming any more,' said David.

'What?' said Stephanie.

'The heater at the pool's bust. Water's freezing. We can't go in.'

'And Mr Livingstone's got a new car,' said Joey.

'It's great,' said Jasvinda. 'It's one of those really old ones with funny wheels and a platform on each side.'

'And,' began David. But Stephanie interrupted him.

'Don't tell me,' she said. 'Just don't tell me. I can't stand any more. Three weeks, and the whole place has changed.'

'It's funny,' said Jasvinda. 'I hadn't noticed. But you're right. There's lots of new things.'

'David,' boomed an enormous voice. They turned and looked. Miss Evans was in the doorway, waving a comb.

'Was that her?' asked Stephanie.

David trotted off. They watched while Miss Evans tried to tug the comb through his wild hair.

'That must hurt,' said Joey. His own crinkly black hair was cut very short and hugged the top of his head.

'But she's so quiet,' said Stephanie, whose hair was braided in neat rows, each one fastened with three coloured beads.

'Only in the classroom,' said Jasvinda. 'She can be loud when she wants to.' Jasvinda's hair was long, and black, and shiny and she wound it into a heavy plait.

'So I hear,' said Stephanie. 'There's a lot I've got to learn.'

'You need a newspaper,' said Joey. 'To tell you everything that's happened.'

'Great,' said Jasvinda. 'We'll write you one.'

David's screams carried across the playground. Miss Evans was tugging the comb through his protesting curls.

'First Edition,' grinned Stephanie. 'New teacher pulls off boy's head.'

Chapter 2

'We can write it straight on to the computer,' said David at lunchtime.

He rubbed his head where it still hurt from the comb. For all her efforts Miss Evans had not succeeded in making it one little bit more tidy.

'It can't be too big,' said Jasvinda.

'Two pages. We can photocopy them and sell them as a single sheet. Five pence each. All money into the School Fund,' said David.

'Then we can buy a new hamster,' said Stephanie.

'What do we put in it?' asked David.

'News,' said Joey. 'Everything that's happened so far this term. And we'll do a new issue every week.'

'We need a name,' said Jasvinda. 'A newspaper name.'

'*The School Times*,' said David.

'No.'

'*The Class Recorder*,' suggested Stephanie.

'Sounds like a musical instrument.'

'*The Telegraph*.'

'That's already a newspaper.'

'*The Daily Post,*' said Jasvinda. 'That's a proper newspaper name.'

'All right,' they agreed. '*The Daily Post.*'

'Hang on, though,' said Joey. 'It won't be daily, will it?'

'They can buy it every day,' said Stephanie.

'But it won't be different every day. It has to be different to call it "Daily".'

'Weekly, then,' said Stephanie. '*The Weekly Post.*'

'Great. That's it.'

So they shook hands and agreed it.

They were so excited through afternoon school that Miss Evans had to raise her voice to make them work. Stephanie grew more and more sulky because she had to sit next to Wet Janine. She tried mouthing across to the others, but Miss Evans made her move her chair to the other side of the table so that she was facing away from them.

'I always sat there,' she said. 'Always. When Miss Markworthy was here.'

'And now you sit where I tell you,' said Miss Evans cheerfully.

As soon as school was over they ran to Mr Livingstone's room and banged on his door.

'Right, come in,' he shouted.

They went in.

'Line up, turn round, bend over,' he said. 'Miss Harvey,' he shouted through the door to the sec-

13

retary's office. 'Bring me my new cane. The thin one, with the whippy end that really hurts.'

'Yes, Mr Livingstone,' she answered. 'Right with you.'

The four friends grinned at each other.

'And wipe those grins off your face,' he ordered them.

Mr Livingstone was so tall he could reach up and touch the high ceiling of his office without having

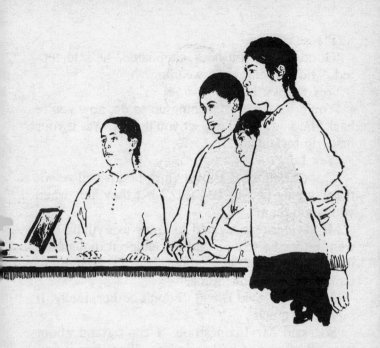

to stand on tip toe. He was a thin, menacing figure with a cruel mouth and grey hair. The children loved him. He had never lost his temper with anyone as far as any child in the school could remember. And though he had never caned anyone in his life he often threatened unexpected visitors with his newest, whippiest cane.

'Mr Livingstone,' said Jasvinda.

'Yes.'

15

'Please may we . . .'

'Good to see you back, Stephanie,' he interrupted. 'Did you enjoy the wedding?'

'Yes, thanks. I . . .'

'You'll have some catching up to do, now you're back,' he said. 'But I expect you'll do it. Was it your first trip to Jamaica?'

'Yes. I . . .'

'Good. And what a lovely lot of curls you've got there, young David,' he said. 'I bet they hurt when you comb them.'

Mr Livingstone seemed to know everything that went on in the school, and the children thought he might have some idea about David's attempt to tame his hair at lunchtime.

'Not really,' said David. 'I don't bother, really. It seems too much . . .'

'So,' said Mr Livingstone, 'I can't stand about here all afternoon with you four. What was it you wanted? Don't keep me gossiping like this, I'm a busy man.'

He leaned back in his chair, picked up a cup of tea and sipped it. He could not have looked less busy.

'We want to write a newspaper,' said Jasvinda. 'About all the things that happen in school.'

'And sell it for school funds,' said Joey. 'Every week.'

'Seems a good idea,' he agreed. 'What will you put in it?'

'News,' said David.

'Do you think there's enough in this school?' asked Mr Livingstone.

'Oh, yes.'

'Tell me five things, then,' he suggested.

'There's the hamster dying,' said Joey.

'And Miss Markworthy's baby,' said Jasvinda.

'And Miss Evans coming,' said Stephanie.

'And the goldfish,' said Joey.

David tried to think of something to say, but he couldn't.

'That's not a lot, is it?' said Mr Livingstone. 'Not for a weekly newspaper.'

They looked sadly at each other. It was a bad idea after all. They couldn't do it.

'I expect you'll want a sports column, won't you?' said Mr Livingstone. 'And you'll do interviews with people to find out about them and what they think about things.' He paused. 'And you'll have features, things like puzzles and recipes and book reviews. And you're sure to have a fashion column. People never think about anything else but fashion these days. Except music, of course, and films and television. You'll probably have all that in. But I expect you've thought of that already, haven't you?'

'Oh, yes,' said David. 'We'd planned to do all of

that. I'm the Sports Editor.'

'No,' said Stephanie, 'I'm doing that.'

Mr Livingstone smiled. 'Well, you'll need to sort that one out, won't you? But get out, now, get out, before I beat you black and blue. Where is that cane? Miss Harvey must have lost it. Go through and ask her to find it, will you? And talk to her about paper and photocopying and all those things. Go on, get out.'

'Yes, Sir. Thank you, Sir. Goodbye.'

They ran out of his office, clutched each other for joy and jumped up and down.

'We're doing it,' they said. 'We're really doing it.'

The door opened and Mr Livingstone's head poked out.

'Stop that dreadful row, before I send for my cane,' he threatened. 'And one other thing.'

'Yes.'

'Make sure you don't write anything that isn't absolutely true. I know that it will make your newspaper unique. All other newspapers have half-witted people writing half-true things about other people to make them sound bad. You don't. All right? Set a standard.'

'Yes.'

'And watch out for Sara.'

The friends grinned and nodded, except for Stephanie.

'Who's Sara?' she asked.

'Oh, you don't know, do you?' said David.

'It was while you were away. A man came and said he'd found an old book or something about the school that goes back over a hundred years,' said Jasvinda.

'And there was something in it about a girl called Sara, who walks around the school at night.'

'A real girl?' asked Stephanie.

'No,' said Joey. 'A school ghost.'

Chapter 3

When they looked at the First Edition the four friends were so excited they just couldn't speak. Except for David, who could always speak.

'It's the best there's ever been,' he said. 'It's monster.'

'Isn't a monster horrid?' asked Miss Harvey. 'Ugly and frightening.'

'No,' said David. 'Monsters are terrific. They're magic. They're ...' He fished about for the best word he could find. At last it came to him. 'They're monster,' he said.

'That's all right, then,' said Miss Harvey. 'As long as you're pleased. You don't look very pleased,' she said to the other three.

Stephanie tore her eyes away from the newspaper. 'No,' she said. 'It's not that. It's just so good I can't believe it.'

'Yes,' agreed Joey and Jasvinda together.

'We love it,' said Joey.

'It's ... it's ...'

'It's monster,' said a voice from above and

20

behind them.

They spun round and saw Mr Livingstone looking through from his office into Miss Harvey's.

'Can't you get these creatures out of here, Miss Harvey?' he demanded. 'We've got work to do before we can shut up for the night.'

'Thank you, Miss Harvey,' said David.

'Thank you,' said the others.

'Can I take one home, to show my mum and dad?' asked Stephanie.

'No,' said Mr Livingstone. 'I don't think so. Someone will see it if you do. Keep it a secret until it's on sale. I'll lock it up in this cupboard. Come and get it first thing in the morning.'

Reluctantly they agreed and said goodbye.

'They seem to have done a good job,' said Mr Livingstone, when the sound of their footsteps had disappeared.

'Yes,' agreed Miss Harvey. 'In the end.'

'Has it been a lot of work for you?' he asked.

Miss Harvey had to put her head right back to speak to Mr Livingstone unless she stood quite a way away from him. She was a pretty woman, with small hands and long fingers. She painted her fingernails a different colour every day and the children always liked to look out for her to see what colour they were. On one famous day she had come with the nails on her left hand painted green and

THE WEEKLY POST

the ones on her right hand painted red. But she was tiny. Hardly bigger than the tallest children in the top class, and speaking to Mr Livingstone could be quite an effort.

'Put it this way,' she said. 'If I had to do it every week, I'd resign.'

Mr Livingstone frowned.

'But that's the whole point,' he said. 'It's a weekly newspaper.'

Miss Harvey laughed.

'Don't worry,' she said. 'They already know how to use the computer to set the page up, but I've had to teach them how to load the photocopier, set it running, how to reset it when it jams, where the spare paper is, and a dozen other things. But they know now, and next week it won't be quite so bad, and the week after that, they'll be doing my work as well as their own.'

Mr Livingstone smiled back.

'Good,' he said. 'Thanks very much for all your time.'

'That's all right. I like having them around.' She picked up the finished paper. 'And, if I say so myself, we have made quite a good job of it.'

'Can I see one?' asked Mr Livingstone.

'Oh, no,' said Miss Harvey, whipping the pile of newspapers away from him. 'Fair's fair. You wait till publication day like all the others.'

THE WEEKLY POST

SCHOOL GHOST SHOCK — HUNT STARTS FOR SARA

Upfield School was rocked with news of strange happenings.

Mr Arthur Clenham, a local man, and an old boy of the school, remembers the story of Sara Martin, aged nine, who was a pupil in the school in 1881.

Sara was killed tragically when fire swept through the school.

For many years, people alone in the building reported hearing mysterious bumps and sudden noises.

Nothing has been heard for many years. Mr Clenham is eager to hear from anyone who may be able to tell him more about Sara's story.

Do you know anything? Does your grandma remember?

Please let the editors know.

Upfield School in 1881

RUSTBUCKET REPLACED AT LAST

A major danger to the roads of Upfield has disappeared now that Mr Livingstone has sold his Rustbucket and bought a new car.

The car, a 1945 Riley, is new only to Mr Livingstone, and has had thirty previous owners, but it is in excellent condition and Mr Livingstone says, 'I love this car and believe it will still be good for another fifty years.'

HAPPY MOTORING!

SOCK IT TO ME

Reporters have made the exciting discovery that there is no mention of the colour of socks in the school uniform list.

The general idea that socks have to be grey is not based on any written rule, but is entirely the whim of the Headmaster, Mr Livingstone.

From today, pupils should wear socks of any colour they choose - there is nothing to stop you.

So, come on, let's see some special socks!

Watch this space for more uniform news.

OBITUARY: PEANUTS

Peanuts the hamster died quietly in his sleep after a long and happy life in Class 6M. Peanuts was a cheerful and helpful member of the class, who hardly ever bit anyone, and then only when he was disturbed. His favourite food of sunflower seeds and a dandelion leaf made up his last meal. He will be sadly missed.
R.I.P.

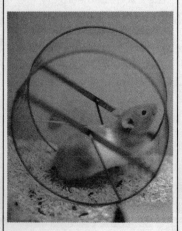

STAFF NEWS

We were all very sad when Class 6M and the rest of the school said goodbye to Miss Markworthy when she left at the beginning of this term to have a baby. Her drama lessons were famous and most popular. And she was a wonderful singer and pianist, usually playing the right notes. We all wish her the very best, and we hope to see her and her baby soon.

Miss Markworthy's replacement is Miss Evans. We welcome her to our school. Miss Evans likes goldfish.

COLD BATHS

The heating system has failed at Upfield Baths and they have closed. Many parents fear that their children will never learn to swim and will be in constant danger of drowning whenever they go to the seaside.

If you are concerned about this issue, please sign the petition by the front door of the school. Thank you.

'Oh, all right,' he agreed. 'But I hope you haven't let them put anything about me in it.'

'You wait and see,' she smiled.

He went back into his study. Miss Harvey picked up the top copy and looked at it with satisfaction.

'That'll do,' she said. 'That'll do nicely.' And she locked the whole pile away in her cupboard.

Chapter 4

Mr Livingstone greeted Joey, Stephanie and Jasvinda with a grimace. 'What do you want?' he barked.

'You know,' said Jasvinda.

'You've come to be thrashed,' he said. 'All right, then.'

'Please, open the cupboard,' said Stephanie. 'We've got to be at the door to sell them when people come in.'

'And who are you?' asked Mr Livingstone. 'Sports reporter?'

'No,' said Stephanie. 'Joey ended up doing that.'

'Well?'

'I'm book reviewer, and features editor.'

'I'm motoring correspondent and local news,' said Jasvinda.

David flung the door open and nearly fell in. His hair was quite tidy.

'You look smart,' said Mr Livingstone. 'Been to the hairdresser?' David put his hand to his curls.

'Eh? No. I got out in a hurry,' he said. 'Forgot to

brush my hair. Does it look awful?'

'No,' said Mr Livingstone. 'There's a mystery for you. It starts off all right and gets worse the more you do to it. Quite the opposite to the rest of us. Scientists baffled.'

'Please,' said Stephanie. 'Please let us have it.'

'Where's that cane?' wondered Mr Livingstone. 'Then I can let you have it.'

'The cupboard,' Joey ordered him. 'Open it up.'

'Oh, that,' said Mr Livingstone. 'All right.' He jangled a big bunch of keys and opened the cupboard quite quickly, having decided he had teased them enough. 'I'll have the first copy,' he said. 'Here's my five pence.'

David stooped down to pick up a plastic container to put the money in.

'Here,' said Mr Livingstone. 'What's that you're wearing?' He looked at Stephanie and Joey and Jasvinda. 'And the rest of you. I hadn't noticed.'

'It's in the paper,' said David. He grabbed the five pence and made a rush through the door.

'Read all about it,' said Jasvinda, thrusting a copy of the paper into Mr Livingstone's hand. Stephanie scooped up the rest of the pile and dashed out with the others.

The last Mr Livingstone saw of Joey was a flash of bright orange socks. 'Did you see that?' he asked Miss Harvey who dodged round them and came in.

'Yes. Quite a rush. They're very excited.'

'Now, let's see,' said the Head. 'What's all this?'
He looked at the back page of the newspaper, glancing at the items. 'Seems all right.' Then he turned
to the front page. 'Here,' he said. 'We can't have
this. What on earth made you let them do a thing
like this?'

'It's only a bit of a joke,' said Miss Harvey. 'They like your new car. We didn't think you'd mind.'

'I'm not bothered about that,' he said. 'It's this headline. They can't print that. It's a lie. I told them to tell the truth.'

Miss Harvey looked at the paper. 'But that's not possible,' she said. 'They didn't write anything like that. I promise you.'

'Get them back,' he said. 'And quickly. Before they sell any copies of these. We'll find ourselves in court if Janine's parents get wind of this.'

He stared at the paper and scratched his head as Miss Harvey disappeared. 'What on earth made them do this?' he wondered. 'What on earth? They'll have to be stopped. It can't happen again.'

SERIOUS FALL INJURES PUPIL

Janine Grey, a pupil at the Upfield Elementary school, suffered a serious injury when she fell from a wall in her garden on Wednesday. Janine had climbed the wall to rescue her cat, Nightmare, where she slipped and fell. A passerby was alerted by Janine's cries for help and he scrambled up the other side of the wall to see what was wrong. Seeing Janine he found her parents and they sent for medical help. At the hospital, Janine was sedated before her leg was set and plastered. She is recovering well from her injury, but she will not be back at school until further improvement is noted.

The door slammed open. Mr Livingstone started to demand an explanation but before he got the words out David shouted, 'Who's been messing with our newspaper?'

'Just a minute, young man,' said Mr Livingstone quietly. And they all fell silent. Mr Livingstone only shouted and threatened when he was in a good mood. When he spoke quietly he was dangerous. 'I want to know why you broke your promise to me,' he said. The telephone started to chirrup on Miss Harvey's desk. She appeared from nowhere and picked it up.

'Why you made up a story, when I told you not to print anything but the truth,' he continued.

'Mr Livingstone,' said Miss Harvey.

'Just a minute, please,' he answered. 'Will you ask them to ring back. I'm busy just now.'

'It's Mrs Grey,' she said. 'Janine's mother. Janine won't be in today. She fell from a wall and broke her leg.'

Chapter 5

Four pairs of brightly coloured socks stared at each other in dismay at playtime.

'Tell the truth,' said Stephanie. 'Everyone. Promise.' They nodded. They joined hands in a pile, black on white on brown on black.

'Spit,' said David.

'No,' objected Stephanie.

'Spit,' agreed Jasvinda.

They all turned their heads and spat behind them.

'Now,' said Stephanie.

'I didn't know anything about Wet Janine,' said Joey.

'Nor me,' said Jasvinda.

'Say it properly,' said Stephanie.

'I didn't know anything about Wet Janine,' said Jasvinda.

'I didn't know anything about Wet Janine,' said David.

'And I didn't know anything about Wet Janine,' said Stephanie.

'And I didn't change the newspaper,' they all

said together.

They loosed hands.

'Tell me about this ghost,' said Stephanie.

'I don't remember anything,' said Jasvinda, 'except what I wrote in *The Post*.' The others shrugged. 'How do we find out?' she said.

'Ask the man. What's his name?' said Joey.

'I don't remember his name,' said Jasvinda. 'Miss Harvey told me when I was writing the article, and I threw the notes away.'

'Deadem,' said Joey. 'Something Deadem.'

'No,' said Jasvinda. 'I don't think that's right.'

'We'll never find out,' said Stephanie.

'Why does it matter?' asked David. 'It's Janine we're bothered about.'

'I don't know,' Stephanie said. 'It just seems important.'

The bell rang for the end of playtime. The four friends went to line up with their class, but Miss Harvey opened her window and called over to them.

'Come on straight in. Mr Livingstone wants you.'

Miss Evans looked cross. 'Be quick,' she said. 'Straight back when you've finished.'

Clive rubbed his hands. 'You're for it,' he called after them.

'Clive,' Miss Evans warned him quietly.

In Mr Livingstone's office they looked at the pile

of newspapers.

'I don't know what to think,' he said.

'We've had a meeting,' said Stephanie. 'And we know it wasn't one of us who changed it, and we want to find out.'

'Well, you're in luck,' said Mr Livingstone. 'Miss Harvey kept your original print-out on file. Here it is.' He put the sheet of paper on the desk next to the pile of newspapers. 'I don't understand any of it,' he said. 'Do you realise how difficult it was to do this?'

'Yes,' said David.

'Tell me,' said Mr Livingstone.

'Well, first you have to break in and steal our paper.'

'Then,' added Joey, 'you have to print out a new page on the computer.'

'Good,' agreed Mr Livingstone.

'Then,' said Jasvinda, 'you have to photocopy them, and lock them away.'

'And get out without being found out,' said Stephanie.

'And you can't do any of that without keys, and access to your disk, and knowledge of your file name, and the code for the photocopier, and paper,' said Mr Livingstone. 'So really, it could only be Miss Harvey, or one of you.' He stared at them threateningly.

'It wasn't,' said Stephanie. 'It really wasn't. We've had a meeting. I'd know if it was.'

'Yes,' he agreed, stretching out his arms and putting the palms of his hands on the ceiling. 'I know. I know it wasn't you. That's what's bothering me.'

They looked relieved. 'And the most mysterious thing is,' he added, 'how did the person know about Janine? And how did they get every detail right?'

'Please,' said Joey. 'Can we sell the paper now?'

Mr Livingstone looked startled and took his hands from the ceiling. 'Sell it?'

'Well, it's all true, isn't it? You said don't write anything that isn't true. And we didn't. But the story about Janine is true. You just said so.'

Mr Livingstone sucked in his cheeks and thought hard. 'All right,' he said. 'You can.'

Jasvinda banged Joey on the back in triumph.

'But I don't know why you gave it such an odd name,' said Mr Livingstone.

'It's a proper paper name,' said Stephanie. 'Lots of papers are called *The Post*.'

'But it isn't,' said Mr Livingstone. He pointed to the top of the page. In their surprise at seeing the headline about Janine the four had not noticed the title.

THE WEEKLY GHOST

'Can we go and see that man?' asked Stephanie. 'The Ghost Man.'

'Arthur Clenham? I think you'd better,' said the Head.

'Great,' whispered Jasvinda.

'Monster,' said David.

Joey was the only one who looked at all uncertain. 'Do you think it's safe?' he asked.

'Perhaps not,' said Mr Livingstone. 'So I'll be coming with you.'

Chapter 6

'This is terrific,' said David.

'Better than the Rustbucket,' said Jasvinda.

Mr Livingstone's face darkened. 'I want a word about that,' he said. 'Which one of you wrote that disgraceful article?'

They looked at each other in the back seat of the car.

'Well?' he demanded. 'Stephanie, you're the editor. You're responsible. Which one of your staff called my last car a Rustbucket?'

'I'm afraid I'm not free to talk to you about it,' she said.

'Then you'll talk to my cane about it when we get back.'

Joey started to confess, but Stephanie shut him up.

'It was a fine car,' said Mr Livingstone. 'Not as good as this one, perhaps.' He stroked the wooden rim of the steering wheel and reached out of the window to parp the horn. 'But a very fine car nevertheless.'

'This is monster,' said David.

Mr Livingstone sighed.

'We sold two hundred and forty-three news-papers,' said Stephanie, hoping to change the subject.

'That's twelve pounds and fifteen pence,' said Joey, who was the treasurer because he had the best calculator.

'Good,' said Mr Livingstone, 'you'll need a lot of money, because I'm going to sue you for libel.'

'What's libel?' asked David.

'Saying horrid things about people,' said Jasvinda.

'We said it about the car, not about you,' said Joey.

'Means the same,' said Mr Livingstone. 'You said I was the sort of person who would own a Rustbucket. It amounts to the same. I'll see you in court. I'll get thousands of pounds damages.'

'We've only got twelve pounds,' Stephanie reminded him.

'And we gave that to Miss Harvey for the School Fund,' said Joey.

'Then you'll have to pay out of your own money,' he said.

Stephanie tried to change the subject again. 'Who is this Arthur Clenham?' she asked.

Arthur Clenham's house leaned to one side and

was propped up with a row of wooden beams set at angles like the legs of a spider. The roof had twisted as the house had slipped and it looked like the hat on the head of a drunken man.

'I'm not going in there,' said David. 'We'll never get out.'

'It's falling over,' said Joey.

Mr Livingstone grabbed the knocker and rapped on the crazy front door.

'What's happened?' asked Stephanie.

'Subsidence,' said Mr Clenham flinging the door open almost before Mr Livingstone had taken his hand from the knocker.

Stephanie blushed in shame. 'I'm sorry,' she said. 'I didn't mean . . .'

'Yes you did. Yes you did. Come on in,' said Mr Clenham. He stood aside to allow them entrance, and when they hesitated he put his hand in the small of David's back and sent him shooting in. The others scurried past before he could do the same to them.

'Very kind,' said Mr Livingstone, ducking his head to avoid banging it on the low lintel of the leaning door. Unfortunately, the angle was confusing and he hit it anyway. Crack.

'Mind your head,' warned Mr Clenham cheerfully. 'The door's a bit low.' Mr Livingstone rubbed his head and grunted. 'I'll tell you what's happened to the house,' said Mr Clenham. 'The ground underneath it's slipped and it's falling over.'

They looked around them. The floor they stood on sloped away, so that if you were to put a ball on it it would bounce against the far wall. The furniture had all been attacked at some time in the past. Legs had been sawn from tables and chairs so that their seat and tops were level despite the lurching of the floor.

'It's quite safe,' said Mr Clenham. 'Sit down. Sit

down.' As he ushered them to their seats the floor groaned. 'Quite safe,' he said. 'Quite safe.' They stared at him. Stephanie, who had never seen him before, expected something weird and crazy. He wore sensible shoes, flannel trousers, a shirt and tie which showed above a vee-necked pullover. His hair was neat and tidy, parted on the left and receding very slightly. The only thing at all unusual about him was that if his face had been hidden you might have taken him for an unusually neat and tidy schoolboy in uniform.

He blinked pleasantly at them and smiled. 'Nice of you to call,' he said.

'I expect you're wondering why we're here,' said Mr Livingstone.

'No,' said Mr Clenham, and he smiled again.

'Oh,' said Mr Livingstone.

'Are these your children?' asked Mr Clenham politely.

The Head looked at the two black faces, the brown face of Jasvinda and David's unruly hair on top of his white face.

'Not exactly,' he said.

'No?'

'No.'

'Are you sure you should be with them? Don't their parents mind?'

'I'm their Headmaster,' said Mr Livingstone.

David pushed his handkerchief into his mouth to stop himself giggling.

'So you are,' said Mr Clenham. 'From Upfield Elementary.'

'Upfield Primary,' said Mr Livingstone.

David was crying now.

'We came to see you about the ghost,' said Jasvinda.

'Is that boy hungry?' asked Mr Clenham. 'He's eating his handkerchief. Yes. The ghost. That's right. Have you got some news? I'd love to know.'

'We want you to tell us about her,' said Joey. 'Everything.'

A slow, careful look came over Mr Clenham's face. 'But you have got some news, haven't you?' he said.

'Yes,' admitted Stephanie. 'At least, we might have.'

'All right,' said Mr Clenham. 'But you do want something to eat, don't you?' He put his fingers into his mouth and gave a piercing whistle.

A small black and white dog bounded through the door, wagging a tail two sizes too big for its body. Its pink tongue lolled out of its mouth in such a way that the children knew it was laughing.

'Gordon, tell Dolly there are five for tea,' said Mr Clenham.

The dog yelped and dashed out, thumping its tail

on the door as it went past.

'Now, then,' said Mr Clenham. 'The ghost. No, I don't like to think of her like that. Sara Martin. Shall I tell you everything I know?'

'Yes, please,' they said together.

Mr Livingstone rubbed his head where he had bumped it on the door and he nodded.

'Well,' said Mr Clenham. 'It's like this.'

Chapter 7

'We always used to say "Sara will get you" if we did anything wrong at school. The teachers told us not to say it, and we were beaten if we were caught saying it.'

'Beaten,' said David. 'What do you mean?'

'Whacked,' said Mr Clenham.

'What?' Jasvinda said.

'With a cane. We had to bend over and the Headmaster whacked us.'

The four children all looked at Mr Livingstone, who blushed and looked away, and decided it wasn't such a good joke after all, and he wouldn't do it any more. 'Go on,' he urged Mr Clenham. 'Sara.'

'Yes,' said Mr Clenham. 'That's right. Sara. We had no idea who she was, but we always said the same thing. "Sara will get you." '

'Like the bogey man,' said Stephanie.

'That's it,' he said, with a pleased smile. 'That's just it. You see, Sara would get you if you did anything wrong. But she would also get you if you were in the school on your own.'

'At night,' said Joey, in a husky voice.

'Any time,' said Mr Clenham quietly. 'Morning, afternoon, bright sunshine or dark rain. Any time.'

Joey gulped. A cloud passed over the sun and made them shiver. Gordon sprang through the door, leaped on to Mr Clenham's lap and sat there, his long pink tongue hanging out with mocking laughter.

'Who was she?' asked Jasvinda quietly.

'Well,' said Mr Clenham. 'That's just what I want to find out, and why I came to your school. Her name was Sara Martin, and she was there in 1881. She died in a fire.'

'How do you know?' asked Joey.

'I looked it up in the local newspaper,' said Mr Clenham.

'*The Bugle*,' said David.

'No,' he said. '*The Bugle* wasn't here then. It was a different paper. Doesn't exist any more.'

'What was it called?' asked Jasvinda. But she had a sinking feeling in her stomach and she knew the answer before Mr Clenham spoke.

'*The Weekly Post*,' he said. Gordon laughed. 'It stopped printing about eighty years ago,' went on Mr Clenham. 'Still, you're not interested in that.' They looked at each other without speaking. 'They're all in the library,' he said. 'Every copy that was ever printed. I went through them all, from

1848 to 1881, before I found the one I wanted, the one with Sara Martin's death in it.' He paused here and scratched Gordon's ear. Gordon jumped from his lap and went to sniff round Stephanie, his long tongue still hanging out. His legs were so little that he seemed to waddle.

Like a little pig, thought Jasvinda.

'Go on,' said David.

'David,' warned Mr Livingstone.

'Sorry,' David apologised. 'I mean, please, tell us the rest.' Hurry up, you old fool, he thought, secretly.

'Quite right,' said Mr Clenham. 'Quite right. Make the old fool hurry up.'

David blushed and looked startled. Joey, who had known what David was thinking, grinned.

'There really isn't much more to tell you,' he finished. 'Sara Martin died in a fire in the school in 1881. She was only nine years old. Her family left the area soon afterwards. I don't know anything else. That's why I came to school to talk to you. To find out if there is anything in your own books and records, or if anyone still talks about Sara.' He stopped talking and looked round at them.

Mr Livingstone opened his mouth to say something but before he could speak Gordon yapped loudly, fled from Stephanie and pushed the door with his nose.

A huge woman with very red hands came in,

holding a tray. She looked wildly round.

Mr Clenham sprang to his feet. 'A table,' he cried. 'We must have a table.' And he picked up a pile of books and dropped them to the floor, making a swirl of dust rise up like mist from a calm sea. 'This,' he said proudly, 'is my little sister, Dolly.'

Dolly gave a most terrifying smile to them all, revealing long yellow teeth. She put the tray on to the space on the table and wiped her huge red hands on her apron.

'Tea,' she announced in her booming voice. Standing side by side they were a peculiar pair. Mr Clenham was stooped and grey and only came up to his sister's shoulder. He was grey all over: grey clothes, grey face, grey hair. Dolly towered above him, and everything about her was too big, her hands, her nose, her mouth, her feet. And she was all colours, with yellow teeth, red hands, blue stockings, black hair, and bright green apron.

'Well,' she explained. 'Three teas, four lemonades, a jug of milk and a plate of things to eat. Is that all right?' They nodded. Stephanie thought she would have agreed to anything this terrifying woman suggested. Mr Livingstone stood up politely and gestured to David and Joey to do the same. He stepped forward to shake Dolly's hand. Joey gave an astonished low whistle when he saw that Dolly was even taller than the Head.

The tray proved to hold a plate of chocolate biscuits, a rich dark fruit cake, a pile of iced buns, a plate of bread and butter and a bowl of jam with whole strawberries embedded in it.

'Tuck in,' she boomed. And they did.

Mr Livingstone had a quiet word with Mr Clenham while the children were tucking in.

'I do hope you've got some news for me,' said Mr Clenham. 'Do they still talk of Sara at school?'

'Not really,' said Mr Livingstone. 'Before your visit no one had heard of her.'

'Oh, dear. But is she ever seen?'

'Never.'

'What about the School Records?'

'I haven't looked. I'm not even sure they go back that far.'

Mr Clenham looked very unhappy. 'Then there's

nothing at all,' he said. 'Nothing you can tell me at all?'

Stephanie heard this last question and fished about in her bag.

'There's this,' she said. 'This is what we came to show you.'

She produced a copy of *The Weekly Post* and a copy of *The Weekly Ghost*. Mr Clenham looked from one to the other and then back again.

'Oh,' he whispered. 'Dolly, look at this. Look at this.'

Dolly loomed over him and peered at the newspapers.

'That's very exciting,' she boomed.

'Very,' he agreed. His eyes sparked in the greyness of his face. 'I really think we're on to something here.'

Gordon rubbed himself against Stephanie's legs and snapped at her chocolate biscuit.

Chapter 8

Mr Livingstone smiled, nodded, said, 'Thank you, we'll do that then.' He put down the telephone, made a tick by the last name on his list and then he wrote a short note on a fresh piece of paper.

He adjusted a photograph frame on his desk, flicked an imaginary speck of dust from the glass and beamed proudly at it. 'Miss Harvey,' he called.

Miss Harvey came in and saw the photograph. 'That's lovely,' she said. 'Who took it?'

It was a picture of the new Riley, with Mr Livingstone at the wheel, waving happily.

'Guess.'

'I give up.'

'I did.'

'But you're in it.'

'I used a tripod and a time-delay.'

'Very clever,' said Miss Harvey. 'I think you look splendid.'

Mr Livingstone wriggled with pleasure. 'Still,' he said. 'Business. Could you type that up and put a copy on the notice board, please?'

Green fingernails took the paper. 'Oh, really, Headmaster, you can't,' she said.

'Yes I can. I've just rung round the governors, and they all agree.' Mr Livingstone shook his list at her. 'You don't run this school, Miss Harvey. I do. And if you want to argue I'll get my cane to you and beat you.' He blushed as he remembered his promise not to use that joke again.

Miss Harvey sat down.

'Eh?' said Mr Livingstone.

'What's the matter?' she said.

He sighed. 'Oh, I don't know.'

'Come on.'

'I don't like it,' he said. 'Broken legs, and ghosts, and mysterious magazines.'

'So you're doing this?' she asked, showing him the note.

'It makes me feel better,' he said. 'Doing something. Being in charge.'

'I'll bring you some coffee,' she said.

He smiled. 'Thanks. Anyway,' he added as she made to leave.

'Yes.'

'Serve them right.'

'Wait and see,' she warned him.

At lunchtime Joey shouted out to Jasvinda. 'Jas! Come and look at this.'

Jasvinda read the notice. 'Hey, that's not fair.'

Mr Livingstone popped his head out of the door. 'What's the matter?'

'Nothing,' said Joey.

Stephanie looked at the notice. 'You can't do this,' she said.

'I just have. It took me all afternoon to ring round. But I've done it.'

David moved his lips as he read the words.

SCHOOL UNIFORM

A special meeting of the governors, by telephone, has approved the following amendment to the School Rules:

All socks worn in school must be either a) white b) navy blue, or c) grey.

Signed, J. Livingstone

Mr Livingstone pointed to their legs. Green, orange, yellow, red. 'Starting first thing tomorrow.'

'Huh,' said David.

'And if you're not careful there'll be a rule about tidy hair,' warned the Headmaster. And he disappeared into his study.

'That's not fair,' said Joey.

'How are you getting on with the Second Edition?' asked Miss Harvey.

'It's nearly ready,' said Stephanie. 'I've got most of the stories typed.'

'Come into the office and let's check them through.'

'We haven't found out anything about Sara,' said Jasvinda, 'and it's been a week now.'

'So we're running the same story again. The one that got lost last week,' said Joey.

Stephanie keyed in the newspaper on the word processor.

53

'That looks fine,' said Miss Harvey. 'Let's print one out and check it. You'd better put something in about the new rule about socks, though.'

'No,' said David.

'It might be a good idea,' she said. 'Look.'

David looked at the way she was holding the print-out. 'Oh,' he said. 'Right. I'll do it.'

'Be quick, then we can start to copy it out over the lunch hour.'

They looked at the Second Edition.

'Monster!' said David.

'You'll all be proper journalists if you can keep this up,' said Miss Harvey.

'Let's lock it away,' said Jasvinda.

They all looked as Miss Harvey locked up the copies in the metal cabinet. 'No one can interfere with them there,' she said.

Joey tested the door. 'It's locked,' he said.

Mr Livingstone bounded in. 'Who's rattling cupboards?' he demanded.

'Just checking,' said Stephanie.

Mr Livingstone tried the door. 'That's safe enough,' he said. He pointed to their socks. 'Don't forget.'

'We won't,' said David. 'It's a good new rule.'

'Goodbye,' said Joey.

''Bye!'

54

THE WEEKLY POST

GHOST SHOCK - SCHOOL NEWSPAPER MYSTERIOUSLY RENAMED

The Weekly Post editorial team were shocked to see that its name had changed in the night to *The Weekly Ghost*. The highest authorities in the school have investigated the change but they are baffled.

If you know anything about these ghostly goings-on, please tell our crack team of reporters.

PULL YOUR SOCKS UP

Great news!

The new rule about socks does not say anything about whether they have to match.

Wear one blue sock and one grey one. Or any other permitted combination.

Bring a bit of variety into Mr Livingstone's life!

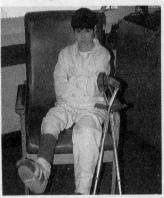

Janine shows us her leg in plaster

JANINE

Janine is making a good recovery after her nasty fall. Her pot leg has a wonderful collection of autographs, and the art gallery in the town is asking if they can buy it for the drawings when she has finished with it.

''Bye, 'bye!'

'See you tomorrow.'

'Don't forget,' said Miss Harvey.

'What was all that about?' asked Mr Livingstone.

'Oh, you know what they're like,' said Miss Harvey with a smile.

'Yes,' he said. 'I do. That's what worries me.'

Chapter 9

The twisted front door of Arthur Clenham's house closed quietly behind him. Mr Clenham wheeled his bicycle along the side of the house, under the wooden legs which held up the wall. Once in the street he mounted the bicycle and clanked down the road. A small, grey, ghostly figure sneaked out of the shadows, listened for a moment, then darted after him.

'Gordon,' said Mr Clenham. 'You should be at home.'

Gordon wagged his long tail and let his tongue loll out of his wide mouth.

'Oh, all right,' said Mr Clenham. 'But keep on the pavement.'

Mr Clenham was rather slow on the wheels, and Gordon needed to do no more than trot gently to keep up with him.

'Soon be there,' said Mr Clenham, more for his own comfort than for Gordon's, who looked as though he could keep going all night.

The streets were empty. The moon rode out from

behind a cloud.

'Here it is,' said Mr Clenham, with relief. He pulled on his brakes, wobbled to a halt, lifted a creaking leg over the saddle, and propped the bicycle against the high railings.

'Oh,' he sighed. 'I think we might walk home.'

Gordon laughed at him. They looked through the railings, across a wide playground and at the shape of a tall building, black against the night sky.

'There she is,' said Mr Clenham.

Gordon looked.

'That's where I went to school.'

Gordon nodded.

'They've locked the newspaper up for the night. If Sara's going to do anything to change it, we'll be ready.'

Gordon yawned.

Mr Clenham looked at him reproachfully. 'Of course,' he said. 'We can't stay here all night. I just thought, that if she was going to do anything, it would be at midnight. It's always at midnight, you know. In the books.'

Gordon sniffed the night air, jumped up, snapped his teeth at a moth, missed, sat down and thumped his tail against Mr Clenham's legs.

'I've got a flask.' He poured himself a cup of coffee.

Nothing moved inside the building. No lights flashed. Gordon shuffled.

'What is it?'

A clock chimed. Mr Clenham counted them all, with his eyes fixed on the dark building.

Twelve.

Nothing.

'Just another ten minutes. To make sure.'

Nothing.

Mr Clenham put away his flask. He looked at the bicycle. Perhaps? He lifted an aching leg. Perhaps not. He pushed the clanking machine along the road.

'Be good to be in bed,' he said to Gordon. 'At least we're sure she hasn't changed their paper this week.'

Miss Harvey was blowing her nails dry when Joey burst into the room.

'Is it all right?' he shouted.

Miss Harvey waved her left hand in the air. The nails were blue.

'Hello,' said Stephanie, following Joey. 'Can we have *The Post*, please?'

'Just a second.' Miss Harvey touched her nails to her lips to test them. Dry. Her right hand – red nails – turned the key in the lock. 'I don't know that I should let you sell it before Mr Livingstone arrives to have a look at it,' she said.

'Isn't he here? He's late,' said Jasvinda, walking in.

'Monster,' said David when he saw the pile of newspapers. 'I ran all the way here.'

Miss Harvey considered. 'I suppose it's all right,' she said. 'If you don't start selling you'll miss people on their way in.'

Joey grabbed the top copy. 'Oh, good grief!' he shouted. 'Look!'

'What's wrong?'

'No!'

'Who wrote that?'

'Not me.'

'Who?'

'He'll kill us.'

'I didn't do it.'

Miss Harvey read the headline: 'I think I'd better lock these away,' she said. 'Until Mr Livingstone arrives.'

'You can't,' said Joey.

'It isn't our fault,' said Jasvinda.

'We didn't do it,' said Stephanie.

They all looked at David. He dragged his hand through his unruly curls. 'Don't look at me,' he said. 'I wouldn't . . .' The telephone rang.

'Hello.

Yes.

Oh, hello, Mr Livingstone.

Yes.

Oh, no. That's terrible.

Yes.'

She put her hand over the mouthpiece. 'It's Mr Livingstone. He can't come in this morning because his car's been stolen. He's got the police with him now.'

'Have they found it?' asked Stephanie.

'No.'

'Tell them to look at the old gravel pit,' she said.

THE WEEKLY GHOST

NEW CAR STOLEN!

The Headmaster's new car was stolen last night, and driven away by joyriders.

After a frantic search, police received a tip off that the car had been dumped in the disused quarry over by the railway sidings.

The car was unharmed except for a mess of chip papers in the back seat.

Mr Livingstone said, 'I don't know why they call it joyriding, it's theft. Where's the joy in stealing a car?'

PULL YOUR SOCKS UP

Great news!

The new rule about socks does not say anything about whether they have to match.

Wear one blue sock and one grey one. Or any other permitted combination.

Bring a bit of variety into Mr Livingstone's life!

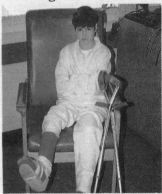

Janine shows us her leg in plaster

JANINE

Janine is making a good recovery after her nasty fall. Her pot leg has a wonderful collection of autographs, and the art gallery in the town is asking if they can buy it for the drawings when she has finished with it.

She pointed to the paper.

Miss Harvey read it swiftly.

'Mr Livingstone,' she said. 'Try the old gravel pit. Yes. Yes. Goodbye.'

'You'd better start selling those,' she told the children.

'Yes!' shouted David.

They grabbed the copies of the newspaper.

'And you'd better be right,' she added.

'We are,' said Stephanie as they ran out. 'We are.'

'I'm sure you are,' agreed Miss Harvey as she read the full story.

Chapter 10

The children all cheered when Mr Livingstone drove the new Riley into the car park the next day. He waved, but his face was solemn and he could not smile.

'It's all right, then,' said Miss Harvey.

'Joyriders,' he said. 'What joy is there in stealing cars, I'd like to know.'

'No damage done?' she asked.

'Not a scratch. They just drove it till it ran out of petrol and left it at the gravel pit. Back seat's full of chip papers.'

'That's good.'

'But a whole day at the police station. Making a statement, looking at pictures of villains, filling in forms. It's no joke.'

Clive knocked on the door and put the register in its slot in Miss Harvey's office. 'Glad the car's back,' he said.

'Thanks,' said Mr Livingstone.

Clive turned to go. 'Hey! What's this?'

'What?'

'The socks.'

Clive looked down at his legs. He wore one white sock, one blue one. 'School colours,' he said.

'They're supposed to match.'

Miss Harvey handed Mr Livingstone *The Weekly Post* and pointed to the right-hand side of the page.

PULL YOUR SOCKS UP

Great news!
The new rule about socks does not say anything about whether they have to match.
Wear one blue sock and one grey one.
Or any other permitted combination.
Bring a bit of variety into Mr Livingstone's life!

'Get out,' said Mr Livingstone to Clive. 'Get out before I, er, that is, I mean, er. Oh, get out!'

Clive darted out. The other registers arrived. Everyone was in odd socks.

'We'll have to do something about this,' said Mr Livingstone. 'Give Mr Clenham a ring, will you?'

'I stood outside the school and watched,' said Mr Clenham. 'There was no light, no movement, nothing.'

'All night?' asked Miss Harvey.

'No, just till midnight.'

Joey crossed his legs, one blue sock over one white one.

'So she could have come later,' he said.

'Or earlier,' said Stephanie.

There was an excited buzz of guessing. Mr Livingstone tapped his pen on his desk to call for silence.

'Aren't you going to thrash us?' asked David.

'Do you still do that?' said Mr Clenham.

Gordon laughed.

Mr Livingstone blushed. 'Let's get on,' he said.

They looked at him, waiting. There was a silence. 'Well, I don't know,' he said.

'Perhaps it wasn't Sara,' said Jasvinda.

'There's no other explanation,' said Mr Clenham. 'It must be her.'

'Think of other things,' said Mr Livingstone. 'Anything.'

'Miss Harvey did it,' said Joey.

'She's got a key,' said Jasvinda.

'I have,' Miss Harvey admitted. 'But I didn't do it.'

'Sleepwalking,' said David. 'She did it in her sleep.'

'You did it,' said Mr Clenham, pointing to the Headmaster. 'You've got a key.'

'Why should I?'

'Because we wouldn't let you see it,' said Miss Harvey, wagging a pink fingernail at him.

'Yes,' said Stephanie.

'Monster!' said David. He whipped out a note-book and scribbled – Headmaster Breaks Into His Own School.

'Wait a minute,' said Mr Livingstone.

'And you stole your own car,' shouted Joey. 'That's how you knew to change the front page.'

Mr Livingstone squirmed with embarrassment.

'You drove it to the gravel pit, and dumped it. Then you wrote the story and changed the paper,' said David, still writing furiously.

'Stop!' shouted the Headmaster.

'Simple,' said David, snapping his notebook shut.

'It's the only answer,' said Stephanie.

Mr Livingstone groaned.

'I don't think so,' said Jasvinda.

Joey pulled a face. 'Why not?'

'Janine. How could he know about that?'

David ripped the page out of his notebook. 'That's a shame,' he said.

'David,' said Miss Harvey, 'don't you think it's good that Mr Livingstone isn't a car thief and a burglar and a fraud?'

David hesitated. 'It was a good story,' he said. 'I'd like to write it.'

Miss Harvey pursed her lips. 'You'll make a good

journalist,' she said.

'What are we to do?' asked Mr Livingstone.

'Well,' said Mr Clenham. 'She's done no harm, has she? So I vote we try to find out more about Sara and wait and see.'

'There's nothing we can do,' said Miss Harvey.

'I can close down this newspaper,' said Mr Livingstone, grimly. 'That's what started this trouble.'

There was a general shout of protest. 'All right. All right,' he shouted. 'You can carry on.' He stood up and put his hands on the ceiling. 'Now get out of here, all of you, before, oh, no. You know. Oh, get out. Get out.' He glared at them.

They hurried out, into Miss Harvey's office.

'That was a bit fierce,' said Mr Clenham.

'No,' said David.

'No?'

'No, it means he's feeling better,' said Jasvinda.

'Still,' said Miss Harvey. 'You'd better get to work on the next edition.'

'What will that bring?' asked Joey.

The door swung open.

'You still here?' barked Mr Livingstone. 'Miss Harvey. Put this on the notice board, will you?' He grinned at the children. 'And read well, or ...' He swished an imaginary cane through the air.

SCHOOL UNIFORM

By order of the Headmaster, the following change to the School Rules comes into effect from tomorrow morning:

All socks worn to school must be of the approved colours and must be a matching pair.

Signed, J. Livingstone

'Never mind,' said Miss Harvey. 'It was fun while it lasted. Better get to work on the Third Edition.' Gordon laughed.

Chapter 11

Joey chewed his pencil and looked glum. Miss Harvey typed quietly.

'What's the matter?' asked Stephanie.

'Look at this.' Joey tossed a large sheet of paper at her. 'We haven't got a headline,' he said. 'There's nothing to put.'

'Run the Sara story again,' said Stephanie.

'That's just it,' said Joey. 'We can't. Mr Livingstone says so.'

'Why?'

'He says that we're asking her to do something by mentioning her. We mustn't say a word about Sara.'

'The rest's all right.'

'But it's not enough, is it?'

'I suppose not.'

They stared at the gaping hole in the front page.

'The swimming pool's working again.'

'That's not a big story.'

'Ssh. The phone's ringing.' They lowered their voices while Miss Harvey dealt with the call.

'I think we should give it up.'

'What?'

'It's only been trouble.'

'We can't stop.'

'And there's nothing to put this week that we don't all know about already, so why . . .'

'Joey!' called Miss Harvey.

'Yes.'

'Would you like to take this call?'

'For me?'

'Well, for *The Weekly Post*, I think.'

Joey took the phone. 'Hello. Yes it is. Who's that?' He put his hand over the mouthpiece. 'It's Miss Markworthy.'

Stephanie leaped to his side.

'Yes,' he said. 'Yes. That's great. Great. What's her name?' He scribbled 'Lucy' in his notebook. 'How much?' He scribbled '6lbs 12oz'. 'Wonderful. Great. Thank you. Yes.' He put the phone down. 'Hold the front page,' he said.

Mr Livingstone looked at the paper.

'We thought you'd better see it,' said David.

'Just to make sure,' said Jasvinda.

'We don't want any trouble,' said Stephanie.

'So is it all right?' asked Joey.

'I think it's great,' said Mr Livingstone. 'It's exactly what we need.' They all grinned at him.

'No mention of Sara,' said Stephanie. 'See.'

'Good.'

'So, we should be all right,' said Joey.

Mr Livingstone nodded. 'And nothing about socks,' he said. 'That's good.'

'Huh,' said David.

They locked the pile of newspapers away in the cupboard, left the office, locked that door, then turned out the lights and said goodbye to Geoff, the school caretaker.

It was getting gloomy as they crossed the playground.

'Soon be Christmas,' said Mr Livingstone. 'Then Miss Markworthy will be back.'

'What?' asked Joey.

'Didn't you know?'

'No.'

'That's right,' said Miss Harvey. 'She's only away for this term. Back after Christmas. When the baby's a bit older.'

'Monster,' said David.

'No, it's a nice baby,' said Mr Livingstone.

'I meant . . .'

They laughed.

'Hello,' said Mr Clenham. 'Am I too late?'

'School's finished for the day,' said the Headmaster.

'Oh, I am too late.'

'What is it?' asked Miss Harvey.

Gordon grinned up at her.

'I've found this,' said Mr Clenham.

He took a sheaf of papers out of his pocket.

'Photocopies,' he said. 'Here's a picture of Sara, she's the fifth one along on the front row. And here's a copy of the school's report on the fire.'

They craned over, looking at the old class photograph. The girls were in long dresses and pinafores, the boys in bulky trousers and jackets.

'Where did you get these?'

'At *The Bugle*. It seems that it is the same paper, after all, but it changed its name about fifty years ago. This is stuff they collected for their article but didn't print. It was in their archives. See here. There's more.'

Mr Livingstone looked at his watch.

'I can't stay,' he said. 'I've got to go back to the police station, to look at some more photographs and make more statements.'

'Oh dear,' said Mr Clenham. 'I wanted to give you these for safe keeping.'

'I'll lock them in my office,' said Miss Harvey.

Mr Livingstone pulled the self-starter of the Riley. It coughed and shook, then came to life. 'Come back tomorrow,' he called to Mr Clenham. 'We'll look at them then.'

'I will.'

THE WEEKLY POST

NEW BABY WEIGHS 6lbs 12oz

We are pleased to announce the birth of Miss Markworthy's baby, who was delivered safely yesterday. Mother and baby are both well. We hope that they will visit the school soon.

PUZZLE CORNER

If an electric train was travelling south at 50 miles per hour, and the wind was blowing east, at 30 miles per hour, in which direction would the smoke go, and at what speed?

Miss Markworthy on her last day at Upfield School

PETITION WINS

Well done, Upfield Primary.

The Lord Mayor read our petition and she insisted that work should begin straight away on the swimming pool.

Get out your flippers and goggles, ready for the GALA OPENING next month.

They waved goodbye.

'We'll come in with you,' said Jasvinda to Miss Harvey.

'No need.'

'We want to,' said Joey.

'You're early,' said Geoff, as they all marched past him. 'Can't you stay away?'

Miss Harvey had just got the cupboard open when the phone rang. 'Yes, Headmaster,' she promised. 'We'll lock everything up carefully.'

Joey gasped as Stephanie whipped the top copy of *The Weekly Ghost* off its pile and stuffed it up her jumper.

'All done,' said Miss Harvey, turning back to the cupboard. 'Got everything in there safely, Mr Clenham?'

'Yes.'

She locked the cupboard, snapped the keys into her handbag and shooed the children out again.

'See you tomorrow.'

'Be there early. Get those papers sold.'

'Goodnight.'

Gordon laughed.

'I'll be off, then,' said Mr Clenham.

They waited until Miss Harvey and Mr Clenham were out of sight, then Stephanie pulled out the newspaper. They looked eagerly at the front page.

THE WEEKLY GHOST

UPFIELD SCHOOL DESTROYED BY FIRE

Last night fire raged through Upfield School, completely destroying the upper floor. Firemen are investigating the cause, believed to be a faulty connection in a plug for a classroom computer. It is feared that the whole structure is now unsafe and will have to be demolished. Children will be allocated to other schools in the area.

Upfield School destroyed by fire

PETITION WINS

Well done, Upfield Primary.

The Lord Mayor read our petition and she insisted that work should begin straight away on the swimming pool.

Get out your flippers and goggles, ready for the GALA OPENING next month.

PUZZLE CORNER

If an electric train was travelling south at 50 miles per hour, and the wind was blowing east, at 30 miles per hour, in which direction would the smoke go, and at what speed?

'Wow,' said Jasvinda. 'Look at that.'

'Monster,' said David.

'But what can we do about it?' asked Stephanie.

'We'll have to come back later, tonight, and find Sara,' said Joey. 'She'll know.'

'She'd better,' said Stephanie. 'Or there'll be terrible trouble.' They stared at the headline.

Chapter 12

The school loomed at them in the darkness.

'We'll never get in,' said Joey. 'Let's go home.'

'We can't just ignore the paper,' said Jasvinda.

'Everything's come true,' said David.

'We could ring the police,' said Joey.

'Or the fire brigade.'

'They'd never believe us,' said Stephanie.

'Or Mr Livingstone.'

'They'd never believe him,' she said.

'But he could sort it out,' said Joey. 'Not us.'

Jasvinda squealed softly as something hairy brushed her leg.

'Hello,' said Mr Clenham.

Gordon laughed and banged his tail against her leg again.

'I thought you'd be here,' he said.

Stephanie bit her lip. 'We're just going,' she said.

'Tell him,' David urged her.

'Shut up.'

'Go on.'

Mr Clenham waited.

'It's nothing,' said Stephanie.

'The school's going to burn down,' said David.

'It can't do that,' said Mr Clenham. 'I went there. Years ago.'

Stephanie glowered at David and produced the newspaper.

'I see,' said Mr Clenham. 'We'd better do something about this.'

David beamed. 'Monster,' he said.

'We'll have to get in,' said Joey.

'Yes.'

'But it's all locked.'

'Let's go nearer,' said Mr Clenham. 'And have a proper look.'

All the downstairs windows were locked.

'This should be easy enough,' said Mr Clenham. He opened a penknife and slid it into the crack of the Headmaster's window.

'Learned how to do this when I was a boy,' he explained. 'Easy.'

The blade snapped.

'Oh.'

Gordon laughed.

'What now?' asked Stephanie.

They looked around again.

'There's a window open up there,' said Mr Clenham.

It was three floors up.

'And a drainpipe up the side. You could shin up the drainpipe, climb in, come down and let us in.'

Joey shook his head. 'Not me.'

'What about you?'

David refused.

'I'll do it,' said Jasvinda. 'I can climb.'

'It's not a job for a girl,' said Mr Clenham.

'It's not a job for anyone,' said Stephanie. 'You'd be killed.'

'When I was a boy,' said Mr Clenham. 'I would . . .'

'No,' they all said together.

'Oh, all right.'

'We need a ladder,' said David.

'I've got one at home,' said Mr Clenham.

'We'll wait here and watch, while you get it.'

Mr Clenham seemed reluctant to leave. 'You won't do anything, while I'm away?'

'We can't get in,' said Stephanie.

'Come on, Gordon. Let's get it.'

But Gordon stayed with the four.

'What's that?' asked Joey.

'What?'

'A sort of clank,' said Jasvinda.

'I heard it, too.'

'Round here.'

On the floor, by the Headmaster's window, was the blade of Mr Clenham's knife.

'It fell out,' said Joey.

'Look.' Stephanie touched the window. It swung open.

'He must have forced it after all,' said Jasvinda.

'No,' said Stephanie. 'I was right up close, and he didn't.'

'It's open,' said David. 'He must have.'

'We'll wait till he comes back,' said Joey.

Gordon wagged his tail, jumped, clicked his claws on the window-sill, scrambled his back legs and disappeared.

Jasvinda hopped in.

'Wait,' said David.

Joey followed.

'He'll be back soon, with the ladder.'

'We don't need the ladder,' said Stephanie. And she jumped in.

'Don't leave me here,' said David.

'Come on then.'

David looked round. There was still no sign of Mr Clenham. He sighed, took a deep breath and climbed through the window. Gordon was sniffing at the door and scratching impatiently.

'It's dark,' complained David.

Jasvinda opened the door and Gordon scuttled off.

'Follow him,' said Joey.

'I can't see,' said Stephanie. She peered up the corridor.

'Which way did he go?'

'There's a light.'

A yellow flickering, like a match, danced on the wall, just round the corner at the end of the passageway.

'It's the fire,' said David.

'Ring the fire brigade.'

'Let's look.' Jasvinda set off.

'You'll get trapped,' said David. He hesitated in Mr Livingstone's office while the others followed. 'Don't go.' They carried on. 'Don't leave me here.' He ran after them.

'I saw her,' said Jasvinda.

It was dark again. The light had disappeared. They looked round the corner.

'What?'

'She was in a funny dress, with an apron, and she was carrying a candle. She went that way.'

'Through the hall?'

'Yes.'

'Let's go.'

They felt their way along the wall, pushed open the doors to the hall and stepped in. Light from the moon broke through the high windows. But there was no figure with a candle.

'What's happened?' asked Stephanie.

The hall was cold, empty, echoing. All the paintings and pictures that the children had made and hung around the walls had disappeared. The climbing bars were gone. The piles of rubber mats and benches for gym had been taken out. There was no overhead projector. The piano was the same, but instead of being scuffed and scratched and dusty it was new and bright and gleaming clean, without a mark on it.

'They can't have cleared all the stuff out since we went home,' said Joey.

'It's not our school,' said Stephanie.

'It is,' said Jasvinda. 'But it's not our year.'

'What?' said Stephanie.

'We're in the past,' said Jasvinda.

'No,' said Joey.

'Monster,' said David.

A door slammed. Stephanie sprinted across the hall and out. The others followed.

'Up the stairs,' said Stephanie. 'I saw her, with the candle.'

They ran upstairs, past the first floor, up again.

'There,' said Jasvinda, who had got there first. 'In our classroom.'

'Let's go,' said Stephanie.

'Hold on,' said David.

'What?'

'Well, if she went in there.'

'Yes?'

'There's no other door. No way out.'

'Yes.'

'So she'll be in there.'

'Good,' said Joey.

David frowned. 'But she's a ghost.'

'Come on,' said Stephanie.

There was a wailing outside the window, and a great racket of shouting, and a sobbing noise, loud and shrill.

Jasvinda led the way. David ran to keep up with her. Their classroom was neat and tidy. Desks stood in rows, instead of grouped in fours. Inkwells, which had long been stuffed with chewing gum, and paper and pencil sharpenings, were tidily filled with gleaming porcelain inkpots. The walls had no paintings of work by children, but a map of the world, coloured mostly pink, and a picture in a frame of a plump lady with her hair in a bun and a cross look on her face.

David walked over to the paint sink. It was gleaming white and spotless.

'This isn't right,' he began.

'Ssh,' said Stephanie.

In the corner, a small girl, about their age, sat at a desk copying letters into a book. She was using a wooden pen with an iron nib, and she dipped it carefully into the inkpot from time to time. She seemed not to see them. Her hair was pulled back, like the lady's in the picture. Her skirt was covered by a pinafore, with just a few small splashes of ink on it.

'Sara Martin?' said Jasvinda.

The girl looked around, scratched her head with the end of the pen, and carried on.

'She doesn't know we're here,' said Joey.

'Where are the other children?' asked Stephanie.

'But she led us here,' said David.

'Unless,' said Jasvinda. 'Unless her ghost led us here, but she's still alive. We've gone back in time and she isn't dead yet.'

'Monster!'

'That would mean,' said Joey.

'What?' asked David.

'That would mean that in our time Sara Martin is a ghost, but that now, in her time, well, we're the ghosts, watching her.'

'Don't be stupid,' said David.

'I can smell something burning,' said Stephanie.

'Over there!' Joey pointed to a pot-bellied iron stove in the corner. Its door had fallen open and a glowing coal had tumbled out and rolled past the fender and on to the wooden floor. The boards were smouldering.

David ran over and tried to kick it back to the safe area. His foot went straight through it. He gaped down at the ember, tried again, again with no success. Then he stared across at Joey. 'You're right.'

A small flame sprang up from the floor. It looked around for a second, hunched itself into almost nothing then uncoiled into a bigger flame.

'Sara!' shouted Jasvinda.

Sara Martin concentrated on her writing.

The flame was now a small fire. It spread out, hungrily consuming the corner of a desk. Smoke went ahead of the flame and began to fill the corner of the room.

Stephanie ran into the passageway, and came back with a fire extinguisher. 'It's back to normal out there,' she said. 'And there's people downstairs.'

The smoke was filling the room quickly, and she could hardly see where the fire was behind it. She pointed the nozzle and hoped for the best. There was a hiss and a splutter. White smoke poured out and attacked the black smoke of the fire. Stephanie walked towards the corner, keeping the extinguisher in front of her.

The door swung open with a crash. David shrieked. Jasvinda jumped back. Joey searched the smoke-filled room for Sara Martin.

'Stand back, kids!' A man in yellow leggings and a dark blue coat pushed forward.

A second man, dressed the same, followed him and snapped on the lights. Stephanie stood right over the fire, which was now just a glimmer of red light. The white gas smothered the last of it and it was gone. She had drowned the class computer.

Mr Livingstone looked anxiously round the edge of the door. 'We'll have to do something about this,' he said. The paint sink was filthy again, and there was no sign of Sara.

Chapter 13

Mr Livingstone looked round his room. It was very full. Gordon wagged his tail against the filing cabinet. Mr Clenham fitted in fairly easily, but his sister, Dolly, no matter how small she tried to make herself, was very cramped, and she made things cramped for the others.

Jasvinda, Joey, David and Stephanie squeezed on to two armchairs. Miss Harvey, splendid in polka dot nail varnish, had to step very carefully to carry her tray of drinks in and put it safely on the desk. She pushed Joey's hand from the arm of his chair and perched next to him.

'I've brought a cup for myself,' she said. 'I didn't want to miss this.'

'Miss Markworthy,' said Joey. 'Can I hold the baby next?'

'Of course you can,' she said. 'But you'd better call me Mrs Burton.'

'Is that new?' asked Jasvinda.

'No. I got married three years ago, but it was too much trouble to change my name. I think I'm going to now.'

'Why?'

'So I've got the same name as Lucy. Is it Joey's turn?'

David reluctantly handed Lucy over to Joey.

Mr Livingstone handed the drinks round and Miss Harvey gave out the biscuits. 'When you're ready,' he said.

Dolly Clenham waved a sheaf of papers. 'Photocopies,' she said. 'From the County Records Office. Arthur was looking in the wrong place.'

Mr Clenham stirred his coffee with interest.

Dolly continued. 'It seems that poor Sara Martin had blotted her work in the morning, and she was kept in at playtime to do it again. The fire started while she was alone on the second floor.'

'In our classroom,' said David.

Lucy reached out a podgy fist and patted his cheek.

'Yes,' said Dolly. 'In your classroom. It was all noted down in full in the School Log Book, and there was an inquest. It was caused by a coal falling from the stove.'

'What's an inquest?' asked Stephanie.

'A sort of trial, where they find out things.'

'And the ghost?' asked Jasvinda.

'The stories started quite soon afterwards. No one ever saw her, though.'

THE WEEKLY POST

'We did,' said Joey.

'I think you did,' said Mr Clenham. 'You really did.'

'Nonsense,' said Mr Livingstone. 'No such thing . . .'

'Who changed the newspaper?' asked David.

'Anyway,' said Dolly. 'Arthur's lot were about the last to talk about her. The school closed down during the war, and when the children came back she'd been forgotten.'

'Until I remembered,' he said.

'I think you brought her back,' said Dolly.

'Perhaps,' he said. 'But I don't think so.'

'What do you think?' asked Mr Livingstone.

'I think she came back because we needed her,' he said. 'To stop the fire.'

'But how could she know there was going to be a faulty wire in the computer plug?'

Mr Clenham shrugged his shoulders.

Mr Livingstone stood up. 'It's all finished now,' he said. He handed out copies of the latest edition of the school newspaper. 'You lot have come out of this as heroes, when really you should be locked up for breaking into the school. I don't know. I really don't.'

They looked at *The Weekly Post*.

'It's monster,' said David.

'I'm sorry that it's not going to be *The Weekly*

THE WEEKLY POST

SCHOOL HEROES SAVE UPFIELD FROM FIRE

Last night, Jasvinda, Joey, Stephanie and David risked their lives to save the school from burning down. The brave foursome was alerted to the danger by a message from Sara Martin, the school ghost.

Mr Arthur Clenham rang for the Fire Brigade, who came swiftly, with their sirens bleeping.

Mr Livingstone said, 'I am proud of these children for their bravery, though they should not have tried to enter an empty building at night, especially if they thought there might be danger.'

The Four Heroes

THE WEEKLY GHOST

We owe a special thanks to Sara Martin for saving our school from fire.

She will be welcome here at any time.

Sara Martin

PUZZLE CORNER

Answer to last week's puzzle: There would be no smoke because it is an electric train.

What goes up the chimney down but won't go down the chimney up?

Ghost any more,' said Joey. 'I liked Sara.'

'We'll never hear of her again,' said Mr Livingstone.

Miss Harvey cleared away the cups, and said very quietly, 'We'll see about that.'